LUCY DANIELS

ANIMAL ARK PETS

Rabbit Race

Hodder
Children's
Books

a division of Hodder Headline Limited

Special thanks to Helen Magee
Thanks also to C. J. Hall, B. Vet. Med., M.R.C.V.S. for reviewing
the veterinary information contained in this book

Animal Ark is a trademark of Working Partners Ltd
Copyright © 1996 Working Partners Ltd
Created by Working Partners Limited, London W6 0QT
Original series created by Ben M. Baglio
Illustrations copyright © 1996 Paul Howard
Cover illustration by Chris Chapman

First published in Great Britain in 1996 by Hodder Children's Books

This edition published in 2006 by Hodder Children's Books

The right of Lucy Daniels to be identified as the Author of
the Work has been asserted by her in accordance with the
Copyright, Designs and Patents Act 1988.

For more information about Animal Ark,
please contact www.animalark.co.uk

1

A Catalogue record for this book is available from the British Library

ISBN 0 340 91786 5

Typeset in Bembo by Avon DataSet Ltd,
Bidford-on-Avon, Warwickshire

Printed and bound in Great Britain by
Clays Ltd, St Ives plc

The paper and board used in this paperback by Hodder Children's
Books are natural recyclable products made from wood grown in
sustainable forests. The manufacturing processes conform to the
environmental regulations of the country of origin.

Hodder Children's Books
a division of Hodder Headline Limited
338 Euston Road
London NW1 3BH

Contents

1

New arrivals

"Let's take Blackie round to Lilac Cottage after tea," Mandy Hope said to her friend James Hunter as they came out of school on Friday afternoon.

Blackie was James's black Labrador puppy. Mandy and James had house-trained him. Now they were trying obedience training. But that wasn't so easy.

1

"Good idea," said James. "I want to see if we can teach him to fetch. He's still a bit nervous of Benji, so it's difficult to train him at home."

Benji was the Hunters' cat. He was just the teensiest bit jealous of Blackie.

"Poor Benji," Mandy said as they walked down the main street in Welford. "I expect he feels a bit left out."

James nodded. "I know," he said. "But it won't be for long — not now your gran and grandad are letting us use their garden. It's very kind of them."

"Gran and Grandad love Blackie," Mandy said firmly. "They're happy to have him there. It's no problem."

Mandy never thought any animal was a problem — she loved them all. Both her parents were vets so she'd been brought up surrounded by all sorts of animals. James looked up at her and shoved his glasses further up his nose. He was a year younger than Mandy but he was her best friend, probably because he liked animals nearly as much as she did!

2

"Bye, Mandy! Bye, James!" Sarah Drummond called as she got into her mother's car outside the school gates. "Have a good weekend!"

"Tell Sooty we were asking after him!" Mandy called back.

Sarah and James had got puppies at the same time. Her puppy, Sooty, was one of Blackie's brothers.

Mandy and James waved as Sarah's mum drove off.

"Blackie and Benji will be fine together once they get used to each other," Mandy said to James.

"And once Blackie is a bit more obedient," said James.

"We'll get Gran to have a word with him," said Mandy. "She seems to be able to do anything with Blackie."

James grinned. "Look!" he said, pointing across the road.

Peter Foster, one of Mandy's classmates, was just opening his front gate. He staggered back as a hairy bundle of brown and grey fur hurled itself at him. It was

Timmy, Peter's cairn terrier.

"I wonder if your gran could do anything with Timmy," James said.

Mandy giggled. "I shouldn't think so," she said. "Timmy is something else."

They reached the post office. From here Mandy and James went different ways. Mandy lived in an old stone cottage called Animal Ark at one end of the village and James lived in a modern house at the other end.

The cottage was not just Mandy's home. Her parents' surgery was attached to it, which was where the name came from. Mandy always looked forward to going home after school to see how the animals were getting on – and to check on any new arrivals.

"See you later," James said to Mandy.

Just then there was a rumbling sound and an enormous van came trundling down the High Street and drew up outside the post office.

The driver leaned out and pushed his cap back on his head.

"Can you tell me if we're anywhere near Hobart's Corner?" he asked Mandy and James.

They looked up at him in surprise. There was another man in the cab with him. On the side of the van, in big red letters, were the words Rapid Removals.

"Oh," said Mandy. "Is somebody moving into Hobart's at last?"

The man smiled. "I don't know about *at last*," he said. "But somebody is moving in – if I can find the place."

"Oh, sorry," Mandy said. "If you go down to the end of the road and turn left, you can't miss it. It's a big old house, the gate is right on the corner."

"It's falling to bits," said James. "It's been empty for ages."

The driver looked at the other man. "Just as long as we can get the furniture in, that's all that bothers us," he said. "Thanks a lot for your help."

Before Mandy could ask him any more questions, he drove off.

A bell rang as the door of the post

office opened behind them.

"Now what was that all about?" asked Mrs McFarlane.

Mr and Mrs McFarlane ran the post office. Mandy always thought the post office was the best shop in the village. It sold comics and sweets and all kinds of things. Mandy and James had even got Blackie's first collar and lead there.

"Somebody is moving into Hobart's Corner," said Mandy.

Mrs McFarlane looked surprised. "My,

my," she said. "After all this time. And I never heard a word about it! I wonder who's bought that old place." She disappeared back into the shop to tell Mr McFarlane.

James and Mandy looked at one another.

"Mrs McFarlane hears about *everything* that goes on in the village," Mandy said. "How did she miss this news?"

James shrugged. "Beats me," he said. "Why don't we go and have a look? Hobart's Corner is on the way to Lilac Cottage. I can meet you there."

Mandy ran all the way home and rushed through the door of Animal Ark.

"You'll never guess," she said.

"Guess what?" said Jean Knox, the receptionist, looking up from a pile of forms.

Mandy leaned against the reception desk and tried to get her breath back.

"A removal van stopped outside the post office to ask directions to Hobart's Corner," she said, her eyes shining.

"Someone has come to live there at last."

Jean raised her eyebrows in surprise and her spectacles slid down her nose and off the end. They swung on the chain round her neck as Jean shook her head.

"Well now, fancy that," she said. "And there was I thinking that old house would never be sold."

"I must tell Mum and Dad," said Mandy, jumping up. "Are they very busy?"

"Your dad's got a patient with him," Jean replied. "And your mum has gone to a calving up at Baildon Farm. But she said she'd be back in time to make tea."

"Oh, good!" said Mandy. "Dad tries his best but he just isn't as good a cook as Mum."

"And just what's wrong with my cooking?" said a voice from the door of the surgery.

Mandy whirled round. Mr Hope was standing there, smiling his lopsided smile.

"Oops!" said Mandy.

Mr Hope laughed. "Caught you out there, Mandy," he said.

Mandy noticed her dad was holding something small and furry.

"It's Ginny!" she said. "Is she better?"

Ginny had been a very sick little guinea-pig when she first came to Animal Ark. Her teeth were very overgrown and she couldn't eat properly.

"I've trimmed her teeth and she's eating like a horse now," said Mr Hope.

"Oh, Ginny," Mandy said, stroking the guinea-pig's reddish-brown coat. "Pam will be so pleased."

The little animal looked up at her with its big dark eyes. Pam Stanton was in Mandy's class at school and she had been really worried about Ginny.

"Oh, Dad, I've got really exciting news," said Mandy.

She told her father all about the removal van and Hobart's Corner.

"Do you think the new people at Hobart's will have pets?" she said.

Jean Knox laughed. "Most nine-year-olds would wonder if they had children," she said.

"But our Mandy is more interested in their pets," Mr Hope said.

Mandy shook her fair hair out of her eyes. "Of course I want to know if they have any children."

Jean perched her glasses on her nose and looked over the top of them at Mandy.

"Could that be because the more children there are, the more pets there will be?" she asked.

Mandy smiled widely at both of them. "How did you guess?" she grinned.

2

Jack

"Do you see anybody?" asked Mandy as she and James peered through the tall iron gates at Hobart's Corner.

James shook his head and gave Blackie's lead a tug, trying to bring him to heel. But Blackie had other ideas. He was busy snuffling at the grass verge, searching out all sorts of interesting smells.

"I can see a car," James said. "But the removal van has gone. Blackie, behave!"

"He can't help it," said Mandy, smiling down at the gangly black puppy. "He's growing up so fast and there's such a lot for him to learn. He's interested in everything."

"I suppose so," said James, his eyes still on the house. "I always thought that house looked really spooky."

Mandy looked at the tall, dark building. The paint on the window frames was peeling and the garden was badly overgrown.

"That's just because it's been empty so long," she said. "Dad says the last person to live in it was an old army captain. He moved away five years ago to live with his daughter."

"I don't remember him," said James.

"We were only little," Mandy said. "His name was Captain Hobart. That's why this was called Hobart's Corner."

Blackie gave a muffled bark and began to scrabble at the bottom of the gate.

"What now?" asked James, picking him up.

But Mandy had seen what was attracting Blackie.

"Look," she said. "There's somebody in the garden after all. It looks like a little boy."

"Where?" said James.

Mandy pointed. "Sitting in that apple tree," she said. "He's watching us."

Mandy raised her hand and waved. "Hi, there!" she called. "What's your name?"

The boy continued to look at them but he didn't speak.

"Maybe he didn't hear you," said James.

Mandy shook her head. "He heard all right," she said. "He just didn't answer."

Just then a woman came round the side of the house. She was dressed in faded jeans and a baggy jumper and her hair was tied back with a scarf. Her face was streaked with dust.

"Oh, hi!" she said as she saw Mandy and James at the gate. "You haven't seen a little boy, have you?" She looked worried. "I told him not to go out of the garden. The gate wasn't open, was it?"

Mandy shook her head and pointed at the boy in the apple tree. "Is that him?" she said.

"Oh, there you are, Jack!" said the woman. "You gave me a fright, disappearing like that." She smiled at Mandy and James then turned back to Jack. "Come down out of there. You've got visitors."

Jack scrambled down out of the tree and stood for a moment looking at Mandy and James. He looked about six or seven years old. Mandy drew in her breath when she saw his face properly. He had been crying.

"I don't want visitors," he said. "I hate this place. I didn't want to come here. Leave me alone!"

And with that, he raced off across the grass and disappeared round the side of the house.

Mandy and James looked at the woman, embarrassed.

She smiled at them and drew a hand

across her forehead. It left a long, dusty streak.

"Oh dear," she said. "I wonder if this move was a good idea after all. Jack isn't happy about it."

Mandy and James looked at each other. It was difficult to know what to say.

"He'll get used to it," Mandy said at last, "once he makes friends. Welford's a really good place to live."

The woman smiled. "I hope so," she said. Then she looked thoughtful. "He's going to start at the village school on Monday," she said. "I hope he'll be all right."

James smiled. "We go there too," he said. "Tell Jack he's come at a good time. We've got the school picnic at the end of this term. That's always great fun."

"And we'll keep an eye on Jack at school if you like," said Mandy. "Until he settles in."

The woman looked really grateful. "Thank you. That would be terrific," she said. Then she looked round. "I must go and find him. Goodness knows where he'll have got to now." She turned away, then turned back. "I forgot to ask your names," she said.

Mandy and James told her and she smiled. "I'm Mrs Gardiner," she said. "Jack is seven – he's usually the friendliest little boy. I just hope he gets over this." She looked at Blackie at James's side. "But I don't expect seeing your puppy helped. Oh dear, we've got such a lot of work to do."

Mandy and James watched as she walked away over the grass.

"She seems nice," said James.

Mandy nodded. "But Jack is really unhappy," she said. "Did you notice he'd been crying?"

"And what did she mean about Blackie not helping?" said James.

Mandy shrugged. "We've got a lot to find out about the Gardiners," she said. "And I know the perfect place to start."

"Where?" said James.

"Gran!" said Mandy. "If she doesn't

know something about the Gardiners, then nobody will!"

Gran and Grandad were working on their vegetable patch when Mandy and James arrived.

"Now you keep out of my beans, young Blackie," Grandad said, leaning down to give Blackie a pat.

Blackie looked up at him and gave a short bark.

"I don't know whether that's a yes or a no," Gran said. She looked at Mandy and James. "You two look as if you're bursting with news."

Mandy picked up a hoe and began to weed between the lines of beans.

"It's the new people at Hobart's Corner," she said. "They've got a little boy but he seems really unhappy."

Gran nodded and leaned on her own hoe.

"I went round there this afternoon with a flask of tea and some scones," she said.

"Nobody ever gets to move in round

here without a plate of your Gran's scones to help them along," Grandad said with a wink.

"You know how it is," said Gran. "People can never find the kettle no matter how carefully they packed it."

"And what did you find out about the Gardiners?" Mandy asked.

Gran shook her head. "They've taken on a lot of work with that house," she said. "They're hoping to turn it into a country guest house."

"But Hobart's Corner is falling to bits," said James.

Grandad nodded. "It seems Mr Gardiner is going to do it up."

"Wow!" said Mandy. "That'll take forever."

"And that isn't their only problem," Gran said. "Little Jack didn't want to move in the first place, especially just after his dog died."

"What?" said Mandy, looking up from her hoeing.

Gran nodded. "It was really sad," she

said. "He had a dog called Fred but Fred got very ill and died just before they moved here."

"That's rotten," said James, looking down at Blackie. He bent down and gave the dog a cuddle. "I know how I'd feel if anything happened to Blackie."

"That explains why Mrs Gardiner said seeing Blackie would upset him," said Mandy. "Oh, poor Jack. No wonder he's so unhappy."

Gran looked at her. "Maybe you could

try to make friends with him," she said.

Mandy nodded. "Of course we will," she said.

"But we can't force him to be friends," said James. "He doesn't seem to want us around."

Mandy looked thoughtful. "What if Jack had another pet?" she said. "Nobody could be unhappy if they had a pet to look after."

Grandad looked doubtful. "It might be a hard job replacing Jack's dog," he said.

Mandy shook her head. "I wasn't thinking about replacing Fred," she said. "I was just thinking about Jack having a new kind of pet."

"Like what?" asked James.

Mandy frowned. "I don't know yet," she said. "I'll think about it. I'll have to find out what Jack is like."

"How will you do that if he won't even talk to you?" said James.

Mandy shrugged. "I'll think of a way," she said. "Once he has a pet to care for, a pet that will love him back, he'll be much happier. You'll see."

21

3

Animal antics

Mandy craned her neck, trying to see down to the front of the school assembly hall.

"Who are you looking for?" whispered James.

Mandy turned to him. It was Monday morning. She had been thinking a lot about little Jack over the weekend.

"I'm looking for Jack," she said. "Remember, we said we'd keep an eye on him."

"And we will – if he'll let us," said James.

The juniors were lined up at the front of the hall.

"There he is," said Mandy. "Look, he's talking to Laura Baker."

James smiled. "Maybe he's made a friend already," he said. "Laura is really nice. She's all excited just now because one of her rabbits is having babies."

Mandy nodded. "Fluffy's babies are due any day," she said. "Maybe she's telling Jack about it."

But James shook his head. "Maybe she is but Jack doesn't seem interested. Look. He's stopped talking now."

Mandy watched as the little boy's head drooped. "He looks awfully sad, James."

James nodded. "We'll make sure we see him at breaktime," he said. "And we'll try to cheer him up."

Just then Mrs Garvie, the teacher, called the room to attention.

"As you know we will be having the

school picnic at the end of term," she said. "And I want you all to think of a theme for the day. I'm looking for suggestions." Her eyes twinkled. "Though we've had so many over the years I don't know if you can come up with anything new."

The pupils of Welford Village School had a picnic on Beacon Hill every summer and every year there was a different theme. Last year it had been pirates and they'd had games like 'walking the plank' and 'tug of war'.

Mandy stuck her hand in the air and waved it frantically.

Mrs Garvie looked at her. "Have you got a suggestion, Mandy?" she asked. "Already?"

Mandy nodded. "Oh, Mrs Garvie," she said. "Can the theme be animals? We've never had that one before."

Mrs Garvie smiled. "Animals!" she said. "I might have known that's what you'd come up with. It sounds a splendid idea, Mandy."

Mandy flushed with pleasure as James clapped her on the back.

"Great idea," he said.

"What do the rest of you think?" asked Mrs Garvie.

There was a general murmur of approval from the rest of the pupils.

"I think it sounds terrific," said Peter Foster. "Can I bring Timmy?"

Mrs Garvie gave him a look. "So long as you don't let him off the lead, Peter," she said. "We all know the mischief Timmy can get up to."

"Can we have a go-kart race at the picnic?" Andrew Pearson said. "Beacon Hill is great for go-karts."

Andrew was in Mandy's class. His older brother had helped him make a go-kart last half-term. It started a craze and now quite a few of the kids in the village had go-karts. James had been talking about getting his dad to help him make one.

Mrs Garvie looked doubtful.

"That depends, Andrew," she said. "How many people have go-karts?"

Half a dozen hands shot up into the air, Peter's among them.

"Pam Stanton's got one," said Mandy, looking across to where Pam was waving her hand wildly in the air.

"I wish I had a go-kart," James said. "I'd love to enter the race."

Mandy looked at him. "I thought your dad was going to give you a hand making one," she said.

James nodded. "He is," he said. "But we haven't got round to it yet. Dad's been really busy at work. He hasn't had time."

"I could help you," Mandy said.

James smiled. "Thanks, Mandy," he said. "But I wouldn't even know where to start. And Dad says if I have a go-kart it has to be safe."

Mrs Garvie counted the upraised hands.

"Oh, well," she said. "That's plenty of competition for a race. I think we can have a go-kart race."

"What's that got to do with animals?" Jill Redfern said.

"We can give the go-karts animal names," said Andrew.

Jill grinned. "Peter can call his the *Terrier*," she said.

"Lucky for you, Jill, you haven't got a go-kart," said Peter. "You'd have to call it the *Tortoise*."

Jill stuck out her tongue. She had a pet tortoise called Toto.

Mrs Garvie coughed and gave them a look.

"Sorry, Mrs Garvie," said Jill.

"But Andrew's idea is a good one," said Mandy. "We can have all kinds of animal races. Like hedgehog races where you have to roll."

"And snake races where you have to slither," said Jill.

"I'll bring Gertie," said Gary Roberts. "She can show you how it's done."

Gary Roberts had a pet garter-snake called Gertie.

"Can we have a rabbit race?" piped up a voice.

Mrs Garvie looked down at little Laura Baker.

"Of course we can, Laura," she said. "You ask Mandy about it later."

Mandy turned to James. "We could use sacks for the rabbit race, so that people would have to hop," she said.

"What?" said James and Mandy knew he was still thinking about the go-kart race.

Mrs Garvie looked at the assembled pupils. "You've got a lot to think about," she said. "Let Mandy have your ideas and don't forget we'll need a name for the day as well."

They always had a name for the picnic

day. Last year it had been Pirate Playtime.

"Animal Antics!" said James and then blushed. James didn't usually call out during assembly.

People took up the name and began repeating it as they filed out of the assembly hall.

"Animal Antics," said Mandy to James as they separated to go to their classrooms. "That's a terrific name."

James looked pleased. But he still wasn't as cheerful as usual. Mandy watched as he walked away down the corridor, wondering how she could help.

"Mandy, Mandy, can we really have a rabbit race?" said a voice at Mandy's elbow.

Mandy turned and looked down at Laura Baker. Laura was seven years old. She had dark curly hair tied up on top of her head with a big red bow. Jack Gardiner was with her.

"Hi, Laura. Hello, Jack," Mandy said. "Sure we'll have a rabbit race, Laura. How is Fluffy? Has she had her babies yet?"

Laura beamed. "Not yet," she said. "But she's fine. It won't be long now."

Mandy looked at Jack. The little boy looked terribly unhappy.

"How are you getting on, Jack?" she asked.

Jack looked up at her. "OK," he said in a dull voice.

"I've got to look after him," said Laura importantly. "He's in my class and he's going to sit beside me."

Mandy smiled at the little girl. "I'm sure you'll look after him very well, Laura," she said.

"Come on then, Jack," said Laura. "We'd better hurry or we'll be late." And Laura sped off down the corridor.

Mandy looked at Jack. Then she looked around. Everybody else had gone.

"Look, Jack," she said quietly. "I heard about Fred."

Jack's big blue eyes filled with tears.

Mandy put out a hand and touched his shoulder.

"Wouldn't you like another pet?" she said.

Jack looked up at her and blinked the tears away.

"I'll never have another pet," he said. "And I'll never like living here."

Mandy looked at him sadly. She understood how lonely he felt. Suddenly a voice called down the corridor.

"Hurry up, Jack!" Laura yelled. "You don't want to be late on your very first day."

Jack turned and marched away. Mandy sighed. First James and now Jack. What was she going to do about them?

4

A surprise for James

Mandy sat at the kitchen table in Lilac Cottage on Tuesday afternoon, swinging her legs and thinking.

"And how is little Jack Gardiner getting on at school?" asked Mandy's gran.

"How did you know I was thinking about Jack?" Mandy said.

Gran's eyes twinkled. "Magic!" she said.

Mandy grinned, then she looked serious. "I've tried to cheer him up," she said. "But he just doesn't seem to *want* to like Welford."

"What about him getting another pet?" said Gran.

Mandy shook her head. "He doesn't want to know," she said.

"Perhaps it's just too soon," said Gran.

"Maybe," Mandy said doubtfully. "But don't you think if he had a pet to look after he would feel so much better?"

Gran smiled. "I'm sure you're right," she said. "Now cheer up and drink your orange juice. I've got work to do in the garage and you can help me."

Mandy raised her glass to her mouth and finished her drink.

"There," she said, wiping her mouth. "That was yummy. And those ginger biscuits! You really *are* magic, Gran."

"My special recipe," said Gran, opening the kitchen door. "But you still don't look very cheerful."

"Oh, I've got another problem," said

Mandy as she followed her gran down the path to the garage.

"What's that?" said a voice from the garage. "Did you say you had a problem, Mandy?"

Mandy peered into the garage. Dust danced in the sunlight in the doorway. She shaded her eyes.

"Is that you, Grandad?" she said.

Grandad poked his head out from behind a pile of boxes.

"It certainly is," he said. "In here up to my ears in junk."

"That isn't junk, that's *jumble*," said Gran.

Grandad looked at her and pushed his hat back on his head. "It's jumble to you, Dorothy," he said. "But it's junk to me. Look at this."

He pulled a pram out from behind an old wardrobe.

Gran looked at it. "Well, maybe you're right about that," she said. "It *is* past its best."

Grandad let out a whoop of laughter. "Past its best?" he said. "It was Mandy's pram. Look at it! It's falling to bits."

Mandy looked at the pram. "I can't imagine I was ever little enough to fit in there," she said.

Grandad grinned. "You weren't too little to wreck it," he said. "You never did like being strapped into a pram, Mandy."

"Don't listen to him, Mandy," Gran said. "You were a lively baby, that's all."

Grandad chuckled. "That's one way of putting it," he said.

"The wheels are all right," Mandy said, examining the pram.

Grandad looked at them. "I remember when your dad was a boy," he said, turning to push the pram out of the way. "I showed him how to make a fine go-kart out of a set of old pram wheels and a couple of wooden boxes."

Mandy's head shot up. "What?" she said. "What did you say, Grandad?"

Grandad looked at her in surprise. "What's the matter?" he said.

Mandy was nearly dancing with excitement. "Could you do it again?"

she said. "Could you make another go-kart?"

Grandad scratched his head. "I reckon I could," he said, looking puzzled. "I didn't know you wanted a go-kart."

Mandy shook her head. "Not for me," she said. "For James." And she told Gran and Grandad all about the go-kart race.

Grandad smiled when she had finished.

"Tell you what," he said. "You and James collect all the bits we need and I'll help you make the best go-kart in Welford."

"What kind of things do you need?" asked Mandy.

Grandad thought for a moment. "A couple of strong wooden boxes," he said. "Or, better still, some fresh wood. I've got sandpaper but we'll need some paint. We've got the wheels." He looked at Mandy's old pram. "And I reckon we could use the bottom of the pram to make the base out of. It's a good, solid one. I might even be able to fit the brake to the go-kart."

"What about my old bike?" said Mandy. "It's got brakes.'

"That might do," said Grandad. "Then all we'd need is a guide rope. It's amazing what you can make out of a few bits and pieces. I used to build some great go-karts when I was a boy."

"And you'll help James?" said Mandy.

Grandad laughed. "I'd love to," he said. "It'll be just like old times. I can hardly wait for the two of you to collect up the stuff."

Mandy shook her head. "Oh, I'll collect all the stuff myself," she said. "I want it to be a surprise for James. Just wait till I present him with everything he needs! What do you think he'll say?" She looked at her gran and grandad. "You know what," she said. "You're *both* magic!"

She grinned up at Gran and Grandad. That was one of her problems solved. Now all she had to do was solve the other one.

Mandy was so deep in thought as she cycled past Hobart's Corner that she didn't notice the small figure sitting astride the garden wall.

"Wood, rope, paint," she muttered to herself.

"Hello," said Jack.

Mandy looked up, surprised. "Oh, hello, Jack," she said, coming to a stop. "I didn't see you there."

"You were talking to yourself," said Jack.

Mandy smiled at him. This was the first time he had spoken to her first.

"Can you keep a secret?" she asked.

Jack's eyes lit up with interest for a moment. "What kind of secret?" he said.

"The surprise kind," she said. And she told him about the go-kart for James.

"That sounds great," said Jack, his eyes shining.

Mandy was amazed. For the first time she saw him happy. He looked like a different person.

"So now I'm going to go round the village collecting everything I need," she said.

"Where are you going to try?" said Jack.

Mandy thought for a moment. "I should get wood from Amy Fenton's dad at the timberyard," she said. "Then I thought I might try Laura's dad for nails. He was making a nesting box for Fluffy last week so he must have some."

"Fluffy?" said Jack.

"One of Laura's rabbits," said Mandy. "She must have told you about Fluffy. She's going to have babies soon."

Jack nodded. "Yes, she did," he said,

kicking at the garden wall.

Mandy stopped as an idea suddenly occurred to her. All of the people she planned to visit had pets.

She looked at Jack. He wasn't interested in another pet. But what if he *saw* some pets? He might change his mind. It was worth a try.

"Of course all this stuff is going to be awfully heavy," she said with a sigh. "I don't know how I'm going to manage it all on my own."

Jack looked at her. She could see him trying to make up his mind.

"Do you want some help?" he said at last.

Mandy smiled. "Oh, Jack, that would be really good," she said. "Would your mum let you?"

"I'll ask her," said Jack. "When do you want to go?"

Mandy bit her lip. She didn't want to give Jack a chance to go off the idea.

"Now," she said firmly. "Everyone will be at home."

"OK," said Jack. "I'll run and ask Mum."

Mandy hugged herself, crossed her fingers, turned round three times for luck and danced with impatience until Jack got back. If her plan worked, Jack might — just might — be back tonight asking his mum another favour.

"I've got to be home by six," Jack said as he came running back to the gate, pushing his bike.

Mandy beamed at him. "No problem," she said. "We should have everything sorted out by then."

5

Visiting

Mandy and Jack's first call was at Amy Fenton's house.

"Amy's dad runs the timberyard on the Walton road," Mandy said as she and Jack cycled up Welford High Street. "That's a good place to start if we're looking for wood."

Jack nodded. "Amy Fenton," he said. "I

haven't met her. Is she in your class?"

"She's in James's class," Mandy replied. She cast a quick sideways look at him. "She's got a pet mouse called Minnie."

Jack cycled on, his eyes straight ahead.

"Here we are," Mandy said. "And there's Amy in the garden."

She braked and leaped off her bike, waving to Amy.

"Amy," she called. "We've got a really big favour to ask."

Mandy explained what she and Jack were looking for and Amy went to get her dad.

"Come and see Minnie while you're waiting," she said.

Mandy smiled. She hadn't even had to ask.

"You'll love Minnie," Mandy said to Jack as Amy took them into her bedroom and went off to get her dad.

Jack looked at the little white mouse in its cage. It pushed its tiny pink nose up against the bars, twitching its whiskers and looking at them with bright eyes.

Mandy gently opened the cage and took Minnie out, letting her run up and down her arm.

"You hold her, Jack," she said.

But Jack shook his head. "I think Amy's coming back," he said, turning away.

Mandy sighed. It wasn't going to be easy getting Jack interested in another pet.

"Great news," said Amy coming in to the room. "Dad says he can let you have some offcuts. He'll deliver them to Lilac Cottage tomorrow if that's OK."

"Brilliant!" said Mandy. She giggled as Minnie scampered up her arm and tickled the back of her neck.

"And Mum says Aunt Julia has loads of old tins of paint lying around in her garden shed," Amy finished.

"Even more brilliant," Mandy said. "We'll go round there right now."

Mandy sighed. Amy's aunt Julia was Richard Tanner's mum. And Richard Tanner had a Persian cat called Duchess. If Jack didn't like mice, maybe he would like cats better.

But Jack didn't seem to like Duchess any more than he had liked Minnie. The Persian cat stalked through the garden in front of them as they made their way out to the shed.

"Isn't she beautiful?" said Mandy, bending to stroke the cat's long silky fur.

Jack stretched out a hand to Duchess but the cat must have sensed his reluctance. She backed away from him. Jack drew his hand back quickly.

"She won't hurt you," Richard said.

"I don't like cats much anyway," said Jack.

Richard nodded. "That must be it," he said. "Cats know when people don't like them."

Mandy sighed as she watched Duchess flick her tail and disappear behind the garden shed. But they *did* come away with four half-full tins of paint.

The next house they tried was where Gary Roberts lived. Gary wanted to be an inventor when he grew up so his bedroom was always full of junk – or so his mum said.

"Gary's bound to have something useful," said Mandy.

While Gary searched through his bedroom cupboard, Jack inspected Gary's garter-snake, Gertie. Mandy held her breath. He looked really interested. Gertie slithered towards him, her green and yellow body gleaming. She raised her head slightly, her tongue flicking in and out. Jack and Gertie stared at each other. Maybe Jack would like a *snake*, Mandy thought.

"I knew I had one of these somewhere," Gary yelled from the depths of the cupboard.

There was a honking sound and Jack whirled round, Gertie forgotten.

Mandy put the snake back in her tank and looked at the rusty old-fashioned motor-car horn in Gary's hand.

"Oh, thanks, Gary," she said. "That's going to be really useful."

Jack took the horn and turned it round. The rubber bulb was almost worn through in places and the metal clip was rusted.

"This is great," he said, grinning at Mandy.

"Don't mention it," Gary said. "Any time! Now I thought I had a steering wheel in here somewhere."

"Don't bother, Gary," Mandy said hastily. "The horn is enough."

Mandy was almost in despair as they packed the horn into her bicycle basket alongside the tins of paint.

"What else do we need?" said Jack.

Mandy looked at her list. "Rope," she

said. "I wonder where we could get that?"

"I could chop a bit off Mum's washing-line," said Jack.

Mandy gave him a look. "And get into trouble?" she smiled. Even if she wasn't being very successful with this pet idea, Jack was certainly friendlier than he had been before.

"I know," he said. "Laura said she got a new skipping-rope yesterday. Maybe she would let us have her old one."

"Good idea," said Mandy. "Let's go."

Laura met them at the door, her face flushed with excitement.

"Oh, you'll never guess," she said. "Fluffy is having her kittens – right now!"

"Now?" Mandy breathed. "Oh, Laura, that's wonderful. How is she? How many kittens are there so far?"

"Kittens?" said Jack, puzzled.

"That's what you call baby rabbits," Laura said. "Come and see. But don't make a noise. Fluffy has been in a hutch on her own since she got pregnant and she's used to everything being really quiet."

Mandy and Jack followed Laura through to the conservatory where Mr Baker had set up a separate hutch for Fluffy. Pregnant rabbits had to be on their own because, as well as needing extra feeding, they had to start nest building. And they couldn't do that in a hutch with other rabbits.

Mrs Baker was already there, kneeling down in front of the hutch. She put her fingers to her lips as the children came in.

Mandy and Jack crouched down with Laura between them and gazed at the black-and-white doe. The nesting-box was inside the hutch. It was a simple open-sided box with fresh hay bedding. Mandy could see that it was lined with soft fur. She new that Fluffy would have plucked fur from her belly to line the box so that her babies would have a soft bed to lie on.

Then Mandy forgot everything else as she caught sight of Fluffy's babies – tiny furry little things. They lay there, snuggled into Fluffy's body, their eyes tightly closed.

"Ugh!" said Jack. "They're all wet!"

"Sshh!" Laura whispered. "If you disturb her she might get frightened and she might eat her babies. We must be very quiet."

Mandy held her breath as Fluffy stretched and began to breathe more heavily. Her huge dark eyes rolled towards Mandy as she strained to give birth.

"Come on, Fluffy," Mandy whispered under her breath. "Good girl, you can do it."

Then there was another baby, and another. At last, Fluffy relaxed.

"Five," Laura whispered as Fluffy bent

her head to her babies. "Do you think she's finished?"

Mrs Baker nodded. "It looks like it," she said quietly. "Look at the way she's licking her kittens now."

Laura turned a shining face to Mandy and Jack. "Oh, wasn't that wonderful?" she said. "And all her babies look just fine."

Jack was looking at Fluffy and her babies, his face lit up in a way Mandy had never seen before.

"Oh," she said. "Wasn't that the best thing you ever saw? Look at the little rabbits. They're so tiny and helpless."

"They can't see or hear yet," said Laura. "Their eyes won't open for another ten days."

Mrs Baker smiled. "They've got their mother to look after them for the next two months. They'll depend on her for milk," she said. "After that we'll have to find homes for them."

Jack turned to her. "But who will you give them to?" he said.

"To people who will love them and care

for them," Mrs Baker said. "Maybe even someone like you."

"Me?" said Jack as if he couldn't believe it. "You mean I could have one of Fluffy's babies?"

Mandy looked at Jack, her eyes shining. Mrs Baker examined Jack's eager face.

"Oh, please, Mummy," said Laura. "I can tell Jack all about looking after rabbits."

"Are you used to looking after pets, Jack?" Mrs Baker said. "They can be a lot of work, you know."

Jack flushed and Mandy held her breath.

"I used to have a dog," he said. "But he died. I'd like another pet now."

Mrs Baker looked from Jack to Laura to Mandy.

"I just know Jack would love his pet," Mandy said.

Mrs Baker smiled. "Then why don't you ask your parents?" she said to Jack. "If they say yes then you can be the first to choose, Jack. You can have the pick of Fluffy's litter."

Jack's face blazed with happiness. "I'd like that," he said. "I'd like that a lot."

Mandy felt the smile spreading over her own face. Success!

When they got back to Hobart's Corner Mrs Gardiner was just coming out of the kitchen door into the garden. Jack skidded his bike to a halt and raced across to her.

"Mum, Mum!" he yelled as he ran. "Laura says I can have one of Fluffy's baby rabbits if you'll let me." He stopped in front of his mother, looking up at her.

"A baby rabbit?" Mrs Gardiner said. "A new pet?"

Jack bit his lip. "I know you're really busy but it wouldn't be any trouble," he said. "It's just a *little* rabbit."

Mrs Gardiner smiled. "I think we could manage to give a little rabbit a home," she said. "So long as you promise to look after it."

Jack's face lit up. "Oh, I will, Mum," he said. "So can I really have a rabbit for a pet?"

Mrs Gardiner looked across the top of Jack's head at Mandy. Then she crouched down in front of Jack and put her arms round him.

"Of course you can, Jack," she said. She looked into Mandy's eyes, smiling. "I think that's a wonderful idea."

6
Getting ready

The following afternoon Mandy, Gran, Grandad and James were standing in the driveway of Lilac Cottage. Blackie was busy wrapping his lead round James's ankles. James had his eyes shut.

"OK, you can open your eyes now," Mandy said to James.

James opened his eyes and looked at the

pile of things on the floor of the garage.

Blackie pulled at his lead and sniffed at a pot of black paint. Then he sneezed and shook himself.

"What's all this?" asked James.

"Guess!" said Mandy.

James looked puzzled. "It looks like a heap of junk to me," he said.

Mandy put her hands on her hips and looked at him. "Well, James Hunter," she said, "it might look like a pile of old junk to you *now*, but once you and Grandad have finished with it, it's going to be the best go-kart in Welford. At least that's what Grandad says." And she turned to look at her grandad.

"That's right," said Grandad.

James was standing there with his mouth open. "A go-kart?" he said. "You mean we're going to make one?"

Mandy laughed. "Not me! Grandad's the expert," she said.

"But you're going to help," Grandad said to James.

James turned to him, his face shining.

"Oh, Mr Hope, this is terrific." He looked at Mandy. "Where did you get all this stuff?"

"Oh, here and there," said Mandy. "And I've got more news for you. Jack wants one of Laura's baby rabbits."

"No kidding," said James. "How did you manage that?"

Gran smiled. "Come inside and get a cold drink and Mandy can tell you all about it," she said.

"And then we'll draw up the plans for the go-kart," Grandad said.

"Oh, and Grandad," said Mandy, "could you please help Jack to make a rabbit hutch? There's plenty of wood here. Jack's mum and dad are so busy with all the work at Hobart's Corner they won't have time."

Grandad pushed his hat back and scratched his head. "And I thought I was supposed to be retired," he said. He looked at James. "Come on, lad," he said. "Let's have our break before the whole of Welford starts queueing up for carpentry work!"

James looked at Blackie. "But what about Blackie?" he said. "We were going to have a training session this afternoon."

Mandy took Blackie's lead. "Just you leave Blackie to us," she said. "Gran and I are going to train him."

James laughed. "Do you hear that, Blackie?" he said. "You'd better be on your best behaviour."

Blackie looked up at him and put his head on one side.

"And don't try looking pathetic," Gran said to the little animal. "It's all for your own good."

Blackie lay down, put his head on his paws and sighed.

Gran shook her head. "That puppy might not be the most obedient dog in the world," she said. "But I swear he understands every word you say to him."

"Biscuit!" Mandy said to Blackie.

The puppy was up on his feet at once, trotting beside her, tail wagging.

"It looks as if you're right, Gran," she said. "Now all we've got to do is to try and get him to do the things he *doesn't* want to do."

Grandad and James spent the next week working on the go-kart. James couldn't talk about anything else.

"Your grandad taught me how to use a saw," he said proudly on the way to school one morning. "And he showed me how to cut dovetailed joints."

"What are those when they're at home?" Mandy asked.

James tried to explain but Mandy couldn't follow him.

"Come and see it," said James. "It's looking really great."

So, that evening, Mandy went round to Lilac Cottage with James.

"Wow!" she said when Grandad wheeled the go-kart out of the garage. "That looks great. Are those really my old pram wheels?"

Grandad smiled. "They look a bit different now, don't they?" he said.

"You can say that again," said Mandy,

staring at the long, low wooden structure perched on its wheels.

James ran his hand over the smooth wood of the go-kart. "Those are dove-tailed joints," he said, pointing to the deep box seat at the back of the go-kart.

Mandy looked closely. The side of the seat was joined to the back almost like a jigsaw.

"Now we have to fix a footboard and guide rope to the front," said James.

"A what?" said Mandy.

"It's a bit like a steering wheel," said Grandad. "Or a tiller on a boat."

"Oh, right," said Mandy. She grinned. "Tell you what," she said. "I reckon this is going to knock spots off Andrew's go-kart."

"You bet!" said James.

Grandad looked at him. "Ready?" he said. "We've still got a long way to go if this is going to be the best go-kart in Welford."

James picked up a hammer and a handful of nails. "You bet!" he said again, laughing.

After that, Mandy went round every evening to Lilac Cottage. She was soon involved in helping with the go-kart – and Jack's rabbit hutch.

The rabbit hutch was coming on, but a bit more slowly than the go-kart. Grandad had built a sturdy frame on legs. It stood about a metre off the ground. Grandad was letting Jack do as much as he could and Mandy could see that Jack was loving it. Each evening after tea he raced straight round to Lilac Cottage to work on the hutch.

Jack was as keen on carpentry as James was but Grandad liked someone to keep a close eye on him. So Mandy soon got into the habit of working with Jack.

With Grandad's help, they had glued and nailed the sides of the rabbit hutch together. Then they fitted the partition between the two compartments inside the hutch and, finally, got ready to attach the roof to the sides.

"The roof has to overhang the hutch," Grandad said. "You don't want the rain to get in – or cats either."

"Would cats hurt a rabbit?" Jack asked.

Grandad took a roll of chicken wire and measured a length off it against the front of the hutch. "A cat would kill a baby rabbit," he said. Then he looked at Jack's concerned face. "But we're going to make your hutch cat-proof!"

7

The Cheetah

Two days later, James's go-kart was almost finished.

"There," James said proudly from the driveway. "It just needs some paint now. What do you think of the go-kart, Mandy?"

Blackie gave a short bark and leaped up at James's chest.

"Sit!" said Mandy and to her surprise, Blackie sat and looked up at her.

Mandy gave him a pat, making a fuss of him for being a good dog, and looked at the go-kart. It sat outside the garage at Lilac Cottage, the spokes of its wheels polished and sparkling in the sun. "It's terrific!" she said.

James beamed and even Grandad looked proud.

"I'm pretty pleased with it myself," he said, looking at the finished product. There was an open-ended box mounted on the back with a seat built into it. Mandy looked at the long piece of wood with a crossbar on the end that stretched from below the seat to the front of the go-kart.

"What's that?" she said.

James got into the go-kart and sat on the seat.

"It's for steering," he said, putting his feet on the crossbar and pushing. "It's like a kind of rudder."

Mandy watched as the front wheels turned from side to side.

James picked up the looped rope that was lying across the front of the go-kart.

"And that's the guide rope," Grandad said. "James can control the go-kart with his feet and his hands."

"Wow!" said Mandy. "You're a genius, Grandad."

Grandad laughed. "You're a bit of a genius yourself," he said, looking down at Blackie who was sitting quietly by Mandy's feet. "You've certainly got Blackie well on the way to being the model puppy."

Mandy laughed. "Gran's the one who's really good with him," she said. She turned to James. "What animal are you going to name your go-kart after?" she said.

James stuck a hand in his back pocket and pulled out a picture he had cut out of a magazine. It was a very large cat with a reddish-yellow coat broken up by solid black spots. There were stripes running from the corner of its eyes down the sides of its nose.

"It's a cheetah," she said.

James nodded. "Did you know that the cheetah is the fastest animal in the world?" he said. "There are records of them running at speeds of up to 114 kph. So, if I've got the fastest go-kart, it ought to be named after the fastest animal."

"We can paint it in cheetah colours," said Mandy. "I've got some black paint and we can mix red and yellow to get the base colour. James, your go-kart is going to be the smartest in Welford."

Grandad pointed to the tins of paint piled up at the side of the garage.

"Paint and brushes," he said. "You two get on with it."

The gate at the bottom of the back garden opened and Mandy looked up. Jack was coming up the path with his mother.

"And here's my other apprentice carpenter," Grandad said smiling. "Hello, Mrs Gardiner. How are you settling in?"

Mrs Gardiner came up the path towards them. "I think we're getting there," she said. "But there's such a lot of work to do. I just came to thank you for all your help building this hutch with Jack."

Mandy grinned. "Grandad is loving it," she said. "Aren't you, Grandad?"

Mr Hope laughed. "I certainly am," he said. "Your Jack is going to turn into a fine carpenter."

Jack beamed with pleasure as Mandy turned to him.

"Hi, Jack!" she said. "Where have you been? You look like you've got good news."

"Hoppy opened his eyes today," he said excitedly. "I've just been to see him!"

"Hoppy?" said James.

Jack nodded. "That's what I'm going to call my rabbit," he said.

"Lovely!" said Mandy. "What colour is he?"

"Black and white," Jack said. "Just like his mum."

Grandad looked at Jack. "We'd better get on with this hutch then, Jack," he said. "We want to have it ready in good time."

Jack nodded. "But it'll be another six weeks before I can take Hoppy home," he

said. "He's only two weeks old. He still needs his mother to feed him."

"He'll soon be on solid food," said Mrs Gardiner. "Then *you* can feed him."

"Laura says we can start giving him some solids when he's three or four weeks old," said Jack. "I can't wait to try feeding him. And I can't wait to take him home."

"Then let's get busy," said Grandad. "We want this hutch to be fit for a king."

"Oh, we do," said Jack. "We really do!"

Mrs Gardiner looked at him. "He's a different boy these days," she said to Grandad. "You and your wife have been so kind."

"It's a pleasure," Grandad said. "Why don't you go in and have a word with Dorothy?" His eyes twinkled. "And if she's putting the kettle on for a cup of tea, I wouldn't say no."

Mrs Gardiner laughed and walked towards the house. "I'll tell her," she said.

"Right," said Mandy, rolling up her sleeves. "I'll give James a hand with the go-kart."

When Mandy and James had finished painting, the go-kart looked even more splendid. They stood back and admired it.

"Those black markings look really good," said Mandy. She looked at the picture of the cheetah James had pinned to the garage wall. "Just like the real thing," she said.

James turned to look too. Then something scampered between them both, whizzing in and out of the paint tins. Mandy saw the yellow paint tin rock slightly, then it tumbled over, spreading a pool of paint over the garage floor.

"Blackie!" James shouted.

The puppy stopped abruptly, turned round, skidded on the wet paint and rolled over.

"Oh, no!" said Mandy. Then she started to laugh.

"What are you laughing for?" said James as Blackie scooted off across the garden.

"Look!" said Mandy, pointing. Blackie's coat was patterned black and yellow all over. "He's like a miniature cheetah."

James shook his head. "How on earth are we going to get that paint out of his coat?"

Mandy bit her lip to stop laughing. "We'll ask Mum and Dad," she said. "They're bound to know."

"White spirit," said Jack, turning round from the hutch. He looked a little sad for a moment. "Fred once got red paint all over him. We soaked it off with white spirit and then gave him a good shampoo."

"Just make sure you don't let any of the white spirit get in his eyes," said Grandad. "There's a bottle of it on the shelf here."

"Thanks for the tip, Jack," James said. "I'll just see if I can catch him."

Mandy walked over to Jack and the rabbit hutch. Grandad and Jack had just finished nailing chicken wire on to one side of the hutch.

"I'll help you with the hutch again tomorrow," she said. "There isn't much to do now, is there?"

"We still have to make the doors – one solid and one with wire mesh for each part of the hutch," said Grandad. He looked at Jack. "But I've got a great little helper here."

Jack flushed with pleasure. "Hoppy is going to love this hutch," he said. "I was in the pet shop in Walton yesterday. The owner showed me this special drinking bottle with a tube on the end. You fix it to the outside of the cage and then the water stays clean. I'm saving up for one."

Mandy examined the hutch. What a perfect home it was going to be for Jack's rabbit. She smiled to herself as Jack talked eagerly about Hoppy and his hutch. Jack had certainly changed since Hoppy had come into his life.

8

Hoppy's new home

"Breakfast!" Mrs Hope called.

Mandy raced downstairs and into the kitchen at Animal Ark. Mrs Hope turned from the cooker and put a dish of fluffy scrambled eggs on the table just as Mr Hope came through the door.

"That looks good," he said, helping himself.

Mrs Hope set down a rack of toast and the teapot and settled herself at the table. Mandy looked round the room. She loved the kitchen at Animal Ark with its old oak beams and the copper pans hanging down from them. The red check curtains at the open window fluttered in the summer breeze. Mandy sighed with contentment.

"You look happy," Mr Hope said with a smile.

Mandy nodded. "I'm going to Laura's with Jack today to pick up his rabbit."

Mrs Hope poured the tea and looked at Mandy. "How are you getting the rabbit back to Jack's house?" she asked.

"I thought I would borrow a small animal carrier from here," Mandy said. "If that's OK?"

Her father chewed thoughtfully on a piece of toast. "Make sure you line it with some of the bedding from Fluffy's hutch," he said. "Rabbits have a very good sense of smell. If the new hutch smells familiar the baby rabbit will settle more quickly."

"I will," said Mandy. "Thanks, Dad!"

She looked at her watch. "I'd better go. Jack will be waiting."

"Have a good time," said Mrs Hope.

Mandy's face was shining. "Oh, I will," she said. "Jack is so excited. Grandad was taking the hutch round to help him set it up first thing this morning. I hope everything went OK."

Jack was waiting for her at the front gate when she got to Laura's. She looked at the little boy's excited face. "Come on," Mandy said, opening the gate. "Let's go and get him."

"He's all ready," Laura said as she opened the door to them. "I told him you were coming for him today."

She led the way through the hall and out of the back door into garden. "There," she said.

Jack walked slowly towards the hutch. Fluffy looked up, her nose twitching.

"Hello, Fluffy," Mandy said, bending closer to the hutch and putting a finger through the mesh.

Fluffy wiggled her ears and sniffed at Mandy's outstretched finger. There were two baby rabbits in the hutch with her. They were both black and white like their mother. Mandy hadn't seen the baby rabbits since they had left the nesting-box but she knew Jack had been to see Hoppy nearly every day. Jack and Laura were great friends now.

"Where are all the rest of the babies?" Mandy said.

Laura sighed. "Mum said I could only keep one for myself," she said. "We found homes for all the others."

She opened the hutch door and picked one of the baby rabbits up very gently.

"Look," she said. "I chose this one. I'm going to call him Patch."

"Was it easy finding homes for all the rest?" asked Mandy.

Laura nodded. "Oh, yes," she said. "Once Jack started telling people about Hoppy, everybody wanted one."

Mandy looked at Jack. No wonder she hadn't seen so much of him at school recently. He was obviously making friends – and that was even before he'd got Hoppy home.

Mandy opened the carrier box she had brought. She scooped some of the old bedding out of Fluffy's hutch and spread it in among the clean newspapers in the bottom of the carrier.

"Dad says the smell of Fluffy's bedding will help Hoppy to settle down better," she said.

Laura nodded and put Patch back into the hutch.

"There, Fluffy," she said. "You take care of Patch." She gave Fluffy a pat. "She's so thin and her coat looks really dull."

"That's only because she's used up all her energy feeding her babies," Mandy said. "She'll be back to normal soon."

"That's what Mum says," said Laura. "But I still feel sorry for her. Especially since she's had to say goodbye to all her babies – except Patch." She turned to Jack. "Do you want to take Hoppy out?"

Jack nodded and moved towards the

hutch. "How do I pick him up?" he said.

"Just like I did," said Laura. "He's small enough to sit in your hand. But when he grows bigger you'll have to pick him up by the scruff of the neck."

Jack looked alarmed.

"It's easy," said Laura. "And it doesn't hurt the rabbit. Look!" She reached into the hutch and picked Fluffy up, holding on to the fur at the back of the rabbit's neck with one hand and supporting her bottom with the other.

Jack reached into the hutch and gathered Hoppy gently into his hands. "This is easier," he said.

Mandy smiled. "Well done, Jack," she said as he carried Hoppy over to the carrier. "And if you let him lie along your arm with his head snuggled into the crook of your elbow, he'll let you carry him quite happily."

Jack laid the little rabbit along his arm. Hoppy looked up at him with big dark eyes. "He doesn't reach the crook of my elbow," he said, laughing.

"Not yet," Mandy said. "But rabbits grow fast."

Hoppy pushed against Jack's arm with his back legs. "Look at that," said Jack. "He's really strong already."

"That's why rabbits are so good at hopping," Laura said. "They have such strong back legs."

Mandy stroked Hoppy's black and white coat gently and the little animal settled down.

Laura turned to Mandy. "I can't wait for the picnic," she said. "I'm really looking forward to the rabbit race."

"The rabbit race," said Jack, looking thoughtful. "You'd like that, wouldn't you, Hoppy?"

Jack put the little rabbit gently into the carrier. Hoppy began snuffling round, twitching his nose and sniffing at the bedding.

"I can't wait to get him home," said Jack. "Do you think he'll like his new hutch?"

"After all the work you and Grandad put

into it?" Mandy said. "He'll love it! Just you wait and see."

"Oh, Jack, that's perfect!" Mandy said when she saw the hutch in Jack's garden.

The hutch stood about a metre off the ground on sturdy wooden legs, well out of reach of cats. It was placed in the angle of a south facing wall, just where the kitchen joined the main house.

"Do you think it'll be all right there?" Jack asked anxiously. "Your grandad thought that was the right place."

Mandy smiled at him. "Of course it will," she said. "No draughts and it'll get lots of sunshine." She laid her hand on the felt covered roof. It stuck out beyond the front of the hutch so that no rain could get in. Grandad had thought of everything. "And that's perfect too," she said. "Hoppy will be warm and dry in there."

The kitchen door opened and Mrs Gardiner looked out. She was wearing a pair of baggy paint-stained dungarees and her hair was tied up in a bright blue scarf.

"Oh, you're back," she said to Jack. "Hello, Mandy." Then she caught sight of Hoppy. "Oh, isn't he gorgeous!" she said.

"Beautiful," Mandy said looking at Hoppy. The little rabbit was sitting back on his haunches washing his ears.

There was a call from inside the house and Mrs Gardiner looked round.

"Just coming," she called back. She looked at Mandy. "I don't think this house will ever be ready," she said. "And I've got the first guests booked in for the end of the month." She drew a hand over her forehead. "Can you fix yourselves some drinks? There's orange juice in the fridge."

Mandy nodded. "Once we've got Hoppy bedded down," she said.

Jack smiled. "Animals first," he said.

"If you need some food for Hoppy, help yourselves out of the vegetable basket," Mrs Gardiner said as she disappeared back into the house.

Mandy and Jack looked at each other.

"What now?" said Jack.

"First the bedding," Mandy said. "Then food and water."

"Right," said Jack. "Come and see what I've got."

Jack had collected a whole pile of old newspapers.

"Mum and I divided them up," he said. "She needed lots to cover the floor while they're decorating."

"These are great," said Mandy. "We should put four or five layers of newspaper in the bottom of the hutch."

"And I've got lots of sawdust and wood shavings," said Jack, opening a black plastic bin-bag. He grinned. "Dad's been doing a lot of sawing and I got some from your grandad too."

Mandy finished laying the newspapers in the hutch and scooped up a few handfuls of shavings and sawdust. She covered the newspapers with the mixture and smoothed it out.

"That should do," she said, looking at it. "Now, what else do we need?"

"Straw," said Jack. "For Hoppy's bedroom."

Jack opened another bin-bag and pulled out some straw. It smelled sweet and fresh. He unlatched the wooden door of the sleeping compartment and spread the straw out on the floor. "There," he said. "Now all we need is food and water and we can put Hoppy in."

Jack disappeared into the kitchen and came out carrying a box of rabbit cereal mix and a heavy earthenware dog-bowl.

"This was Fred's bowl," he said. His bottom lip trembled a little.

Mandy looked at the bowl. "It's lovely," she said gently. "And I'm sure Fred would be glad that it's Hoppy's now.'

Jack nodded. "He would, wouldn't he?" he said. Mandy saw him blink some tears away. Then he placed the bowl firmly inside the hutch. "It's yours now, Hoppy," he said. Then he started opening the cereal packet. "You're going to like this."

Mandy gave a little sigh of relief. Jack would never forget Fred but it looked as if he would get over his sadness with Hoppy to care for.

"What about water?" she asked as Jack poured cereal into the bowl.

"I bought one of those plastic bottles," said Jack.

Mandy nodded. "They're good," she said. "The water doesn't get dirty or spilled."

Soon they had the hutch ready. Mandy washed some vegetables and chopped them up very small, mixing them in with the cereal.

"You can give him wild plants as well," said Mandy. "So long as you don't pick them from the side of a busy road."

"Why not?" said Jack.

"Because they would be dirty and covered with car exhaust fumes," said Mandy.

"What kind of wild plants?" Jack asked.

"Oh, dandelions and dock leaves and clover," said Mandy. "But not too much clover. And definitely not buttercups. They'd make him ill. I can show you some if you like."

Jack shook his head. "There's such a lot to learn," he said.

Mandy nodded. "I know," she said. "But you'll soon get used to looking after him."

Jack fitted the water bottle on to the wire mesh of the hutch and they stood back and looked at it.

"Have we forgotten anything?" he asked.

Mandy shook her head. "I don't think so," she said. She frowned. "He'll need a piece of wood or a branch to gnaw on so that his teeth don't get too long. But that can wait."

"So, can we put him in his new home now?" said Jack, bursting with impatience.

Mandy smiled at him. "*You* can," she said. "He's your pet."

Jack bent down and carefully took Hoppy out of the carrier. He stood for a moment stroking his ears before he opened the door of the hutch and placed the little creature gently inside.

"My pet," he said. "And I'm going to take such good care of him."

9

The race

Mandy hardly saw James for the next week. Every spare moment he could get he spent practising for the go-kart race. One day he called round to Animal Ark – to see if she would time him.

"Time you?" Mandy said.

James nodded. "Down Beacon Hill," he said. "I borrowed a stopwatch from Dad."

So Mandy spent the next few days timing James as he raced down Beacon Hill in *Cheetah*. He wasn't the only one. Andrew was there, and Peter and a few other boys including Gary Roberts. Pam and Jill had decided to enter as well. Pam's mum was doing a night class in joinery and had helped Pam with her go-kart. It was painted in tiger stripes and looked good. Gary's was painted to look like a snake. But Jill's looked a bit odd. It was painted to look like a car.

"It was my cousin's," she explained. "I just got it yesterday. I haven't had time to paint it yet."

"You don't have to," said Gary. "Just pretend it's a jaguar."

"Oh, great idea," laughed Jill. "Like a Jaguar car. I think your snake looks really good, Gary."

"It's an anaconda," Gary said proudly.

The air was filled with shouts as they all raced one another again and again.

"Just watch out for the river," Mandy yelled as James raced past her for a third time. "I don't want to have to fish you out."

By the time the day of the picnic came they were all in top form. But Mandy thought James and Andrew were the best drivers.

"Of course you've practised enough," Mandy said to James as they stood at the start line on Beacon Hill. "Grandad says you're a great driver."

James looked down at *Cheetah*.

"It really is a terrific go-kart," he said.

There was a huge banner saying Animal Antics stretched across the starting line. It had pictures of animals crawling and jumping and running in and out of all the letters. The sun was shining and Welford Village School was having the best picnic ever.

Beacon Hill sloped all the way down to the bridge over the river. Andrew, Peter and James had marked out the course for the go-kart race with coloured flags on poles.

"It looks really professional," Mandy said to Sarah Drummond beside her.

Sarah nodded. "Just so long as nobody goes into the river," she said.

"Mrs Garvie made sure the course went in the other direction at the bottom," James said.

The girls looked. The course followed the slope of the hill down to the bottom then turned off in a wide sweep well away from the river.

"Look!" said Sarah. "The go-karts are starting to line up."

"Better get going, James," said Amy Fenton, walking up to them.

"Wish me luck then," James said to Mandy.

Mandy grinned. "Good luck!" she said.

Then Mrs Garvie asked the racers to line up at the start line beside their go-karts. Mandy watched as everyone stood beside their go-karts, ready to jump into them and take off as soon as Mrs Garvie blew the whistle. The seconds stretched out. Then the whistle blew – and they were off!

Mandy stood at the start line with Sarah and Amy, eyes glued to the go-karts racing down the hill.

Andrew, James and Peter were out in front but Pam's go-kart had gathered speed and was catching up. Jill had a bit of trouble as she and Gary veered towards each other. For a moment it looked as if they would collide. Then Jill straightened up and shot down the hill after the leaders. James was neck and neck with Andrew now. It was hard to tell which of them was ahead.

"Come on, James! Come on!" Mandy yelled, jumping up and down.

All around her people were yelling their heads off as the go-karts raced down the grassy slope. First one, then another edged in front. Pam's *Tiger* picked up speed, threatening to overtake *Kingfisher*. Andrew's blue go-kart looked very impressive with its chrome wheels flashing in the sunlight. Then *Cheetah* came up from behind *Kingfisher*.

"Look, James has just edged in front!" said Sarah.

Mandy shaded her eyes from the sun to see better.

"Come *on*, James," she yelled again.

Cheetah sped on, its wheels sparkling in the sun, covering the ground faster than before. James was going to win! He was leaving Andrew behind!

Then Peter's *Terrier* put on a sudden burst of speed and flashed past both *Cheetah* and *Kingfisher*.

"*Terrier's* in the lead," Amy shouted. "Go for it, Peter!"

But then disaster struck. Peter's go-kart went over a bump and spun round right in front of *Cheetah*. James swerved, just missing him. But he had lost ground and they were almost at the finishing line. *Kingfisher* swooped past and crossed the line in first place.

The other go-karts were catching up, as they swept down the hill behind James but he managed to stay in front. He came in second, right on Andrew's heels.

The watchers cheered from the hilltop.

"Bad luck, James," Mandy said.

"If *Terrier* hadn't crashed, *Cheetah* might have won," said Amy.

"Do you think Peter is OK?" asked Mandy.

Jill nodded as Peter picked himself up and waved to the crowd. "Looks like it," she said.

Mandy watched them all trudge back up the hill pulling their go-karts. They seemed to have enjoyed the race.

"You did great, James," said Mandy as James came up. "I think you did really well to come second."

"So do I," said James. "I can't wait to tell your grandad!"

"I won! I won!" Laura Baker shouted, running over the grass towards Mandy.

Mandy looked down at the little girl.

"I won the hedgehog race," said Laura. "I can roll better than anybody else."

Mandy looked at the grass stains on Laura's shorts. "I can see that, Laura," she said, laughing.

Sarah Drummond pushed a trolley full of packed lunches and cartons of juice over to them.

"Mrs Garvie says we can have one more race before the picnic," she said to Mandy. "What should it be?"

Mandy looked at the clipboard she was holding.

"The rabbit race," she said.

"The rabbit race!" Laura yelled. "Wow! I bet I'll win."

And she raced off to the start line. Mandy watched her go. Laura was full of energy.

"I've brought Hoppy," said a voice beside her.

Mandy looked round. Jack was standing there with Hoppy's carrier box in his arms. He opened the lid for Mandy to see.

"Oh, he's lovely," said Mandy, tickling Hoppy under the chin. "And look how much he's grown!"

The little rabbit twitched his ears and rubbed his nose with his tiny paws.

"He can run really fast now," said Jack. "I'm sure he'll win."

Mandy was puzzled. "Win what, Jack?" she said.

"The rabbit race," Jack said.

Mandy blinked. "But it isn't a *real* rabbit race," she said. "It's like all the other races. You have to pretend you're an animal and race that way."

"You mean it isn't a race for rabbits?" Jack said.

Mandy shook her head. "It's for people, Jack," she said. "Look!"

Mandy and Jack watched as Mrs Garvie blew a whistle for the race to start. It was a sack race. The line of competitors hopped across the start, holding on to their sacks.

Some of them wore silly paper rabbit ears. "Oh," said Jack. "I wondered why I couldn't see any other rabbits."

Mandy bit her lip. He looked so disappointed.

"I'm sure if we did have a real rabbit race Hoppy would win," she said.

There was a yell from the finishing line and Mandy saw Amy Fenton throw herself across the line just in front of Laura. When she looked back, Jack had gone.

"Picnic time!" Mrs Garvie called. Soon there was a stampede towards Sarah and the trolley full of goodies.

Mrs Black, James's teacher, and Mrs Todd, Mandy's teacher, started handing out packets of sandwiches and cartons of juice.

By the time Mandy had got something to eat and sorted out the running order of the rest of the races, she had forgotten all about Jack.

She was lining juniors up for the snake race after lunch when the little boy appeared beside her.

"Can I be in the race?" he asked.

"Sure," said Mandy. She looked at Hoppy. "Just make sure Hoppy is safe in his carrier box first."

Jack ran off and Mandy turned back to the juniors again. "You've got to wriggle," she told them. "No running and no crawling."

The juniors looked up at her seriously.

"How about rolling?" Laura said.

"No rolling," Mandy said firmly.

Mrs Garvie put her whistle to her lips.

"Ready?" she said to Mandy.

Jack arrived at a run and slid down among the other competitors on the grass.

"Ready!" said Mandy, and Mrs Garvie blew her whistle.

The juniors started wriggling.

"Look at that!" said Gary Roberts. "Maybe I should have brought Gertie along after all to show them how it's done."

Mandy, James, Sarah and Andrew stood on the start line, laughing. The juniors were all over the place, squirming and wriggling their way along the ground.

"Look at little Susan Davis," said James. "She's gone right off the course."

Mandy looked. Susan had wriggled her way right to the edge of the hill where the go-karts were parked.

"Hoi! Susan!" shouted Andrew. "Mind the karts!"

Susan turned at the sound of his voice and rolled backwards into Andrew's go-kart. It rocked slightly and she put out a hand to it.

They all watched as the go-kart slowly started to move downhill.

"Oh, no," said Andrew. "I must have left the brake off!" He took off at a run after his go-kart.

There was a clamour of voices as people turned to look at *Kingfisher* rolling down-hill, starting to go faster.

Then a terrified voice shouted over the others. "Hoppy!" Jack yelled.

Mandy whirled round as the little boy jumped to his feet and began to run after the go-kart.

"Jack! What is it?" she yelled, running after him.

Jack didn't stop. "I put Hoppy in that go-kart," he panted as he ran. "I thought he would be safe."

Mandy looked at the go-kart racing down the hill – heading straight for the river. "James!" she screamed. "We must catch that kart."

James was already racing towards her but she couldn't stop. If anything happened to *this* pet, Jack would never be brave enough to get another.

Jack was fighting back the tears. "He'll be killed, won't he?" he said as he stumbled across the grass. "If the go-kart goes into the river Hoppy will drown!"

10

Runaway rabbit!

James ran to his go-kart and dragged it to the edge of the slope.

"What are you doing?" yelled Mandy.

"I'm going to try and cut off Andrew's go-kart before it gets to the river," he shouted back.

"I'll get my bike," she called. But James was already heading downhill in his kart.

Mandy saw James race off. His go-kart sped over the grass like a real cheetah. Andrew was halfway down the hill, making for his go-kart. Mandy made a dash for her bike and set off down the path that wound its way round the hill.

Down and down she went, hair flying, legs pumping the pedals. Behind her others raced, all trying to catch up with the runaway go-kart. Mandy lost sight of James as the path took her behind the hill. Then she was back on the same side again.

James had passed Andrew and was gaining on the go-kart. But would he be in time? *Kingfisher* was getting nearer and nearer the river.

Once again the curve of the hill hid Mandy's view. The next time she came round James was swerving towards the runaway go-kart, cutting across its path in a desperate attempt to stop it. Mandy held her breath as she saw James's go-kart cut in front of Andrew's. There was a crash as the karts collided. Then James tumbled out of his seat and lay, perfectly still, on the grass.

Kingfisher and *Cheetah* rolled on towards the river and came to a stop almost at the edge of the riverbank.

Mandy covered the rest of the distance between her and James at record speed.

"James!" she yelled. "Are you all right?"

James raised his head. "Don't stop! Get Hoppy!" he said.

Mandy raced on towards the overturned *Kingfisher*. Behind her, the others rushed up, shouting questions, bending over James.

Mandy leaped off her bike as she reached the entangled go-karts.

"Is my go-kart OK?" said Andrew, racing up.

"Your go-kart can be mended," Mandy said, searching through the jumbled karts. "What about Hoppy?"

She looked round as a small figure came running down the hill.

"Hoppy!" cried Jack. "Where's Hoppy?"

Mandy looked at *Kingfisher*. Had Hoppy fallen out? Had the go-kart crushed him?

Then she caught sight of the edge of the

carrier box, half wedged under a wheel. Holding her breath, she lifted the box up and opened the flap. There, shivering inside the box, was Hoppy. He was terribly frightened – but he was alive!

James arrived, limping slightly, as Jack peered into the carrier box, his eyes huge with fear.

"He's all right," Mandy said gently. "Just a bit scared."

"Hoppy!" cried Jack. He gathered the rabbit up carefully in his arms and looked at James.

"You saved him," he said. "He was heading for the river. You stopped Andrew's go-kart. You saved his life, James. Thank you!"

James blushed bright red. "Don't mention it," he said.

But Mrs Garvie had seen everything. She came bustling up to them.

"Are you hurt, James?" she said quickly. "You were limping."

James shook his head. "I just twisted my ankle," he said. "It's nothing."

"Nonsense," she said. "You're a hero, James."

James blushed even more.

"I bet that's the first time a cheetah beat a kingfisher to catch a rabbit," Peter Foster said and everybody laughed.

Mrs Garvie looked serious for a moment. "I don't want anything like that ever to happen again," she said. Then she smiled. "But since it *has* happened I think we'll award a special prize for the most exciting race of the day."

Mandy looked at Jack. He was cuddling

Hoppy close to his chest. The rest of the pupils gathered round. Jack's face glowed with happiness as he proudly showed off his pet.

Laura stood by his side. But Laura wasn't his only friend now. Jack was one of them now – one of the crowd. And so was Hoppy.

"A special prize would be great," Mandy said, looking at James. "A prize for the runaway rabbit race!"